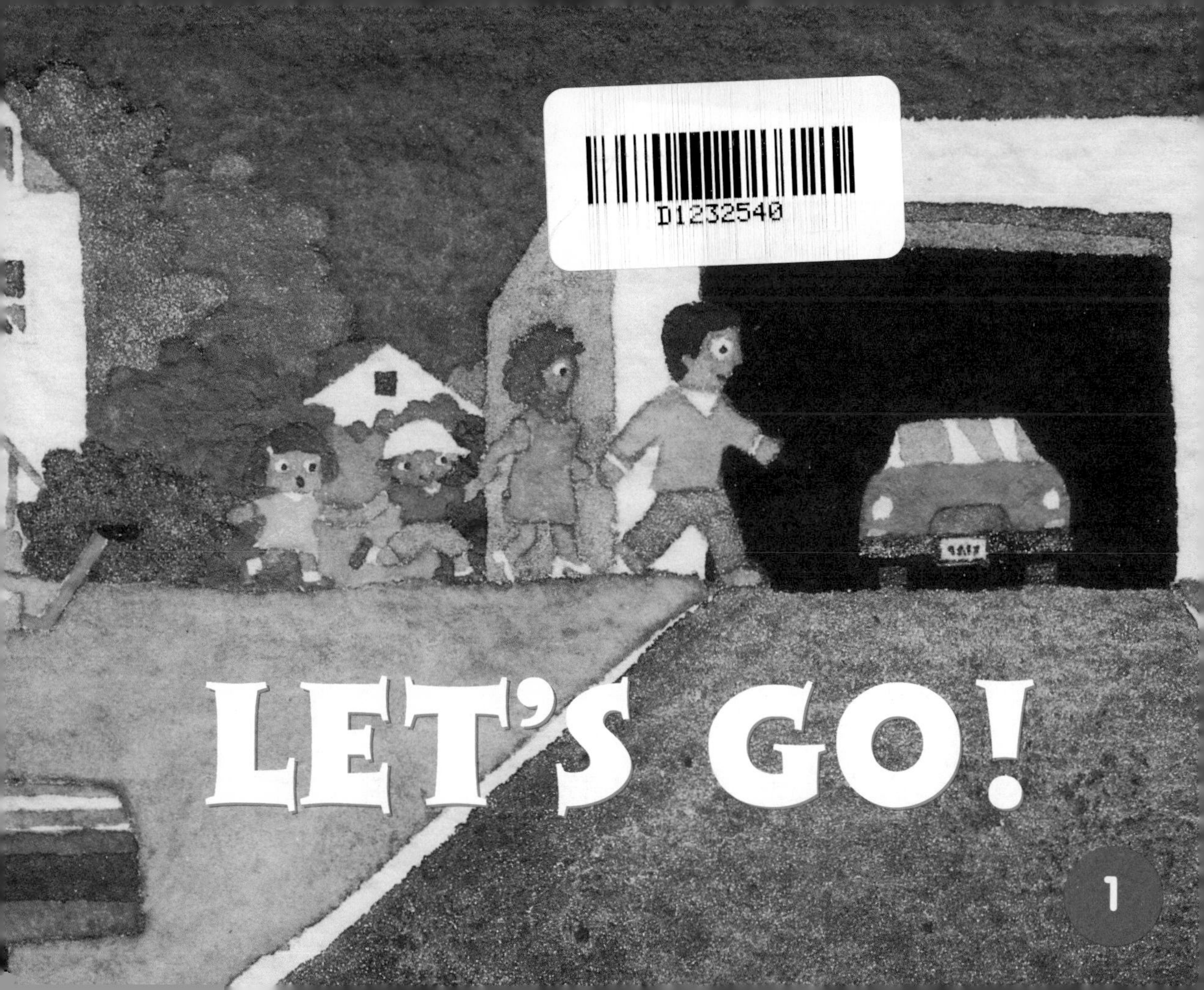

LET'S GO!

1

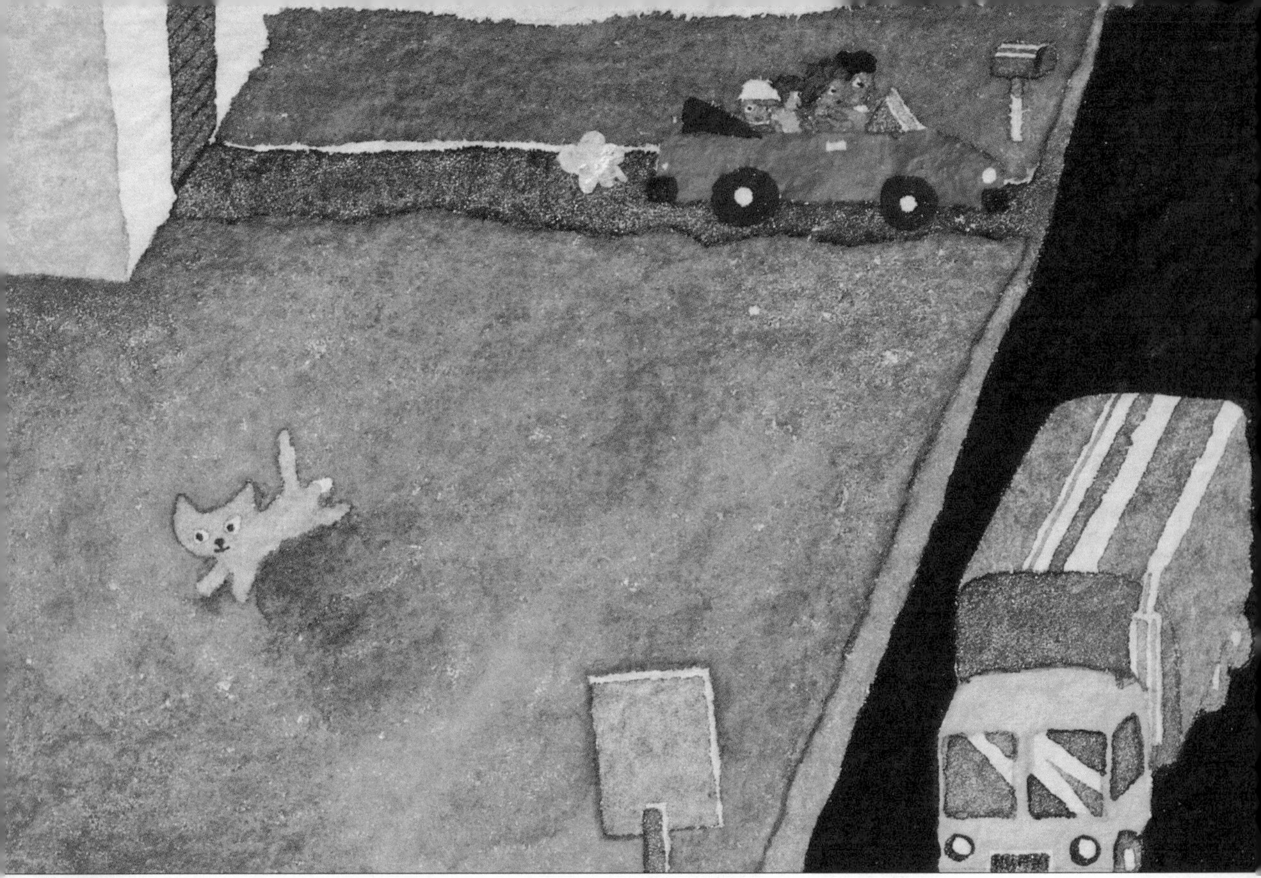

Let's go!

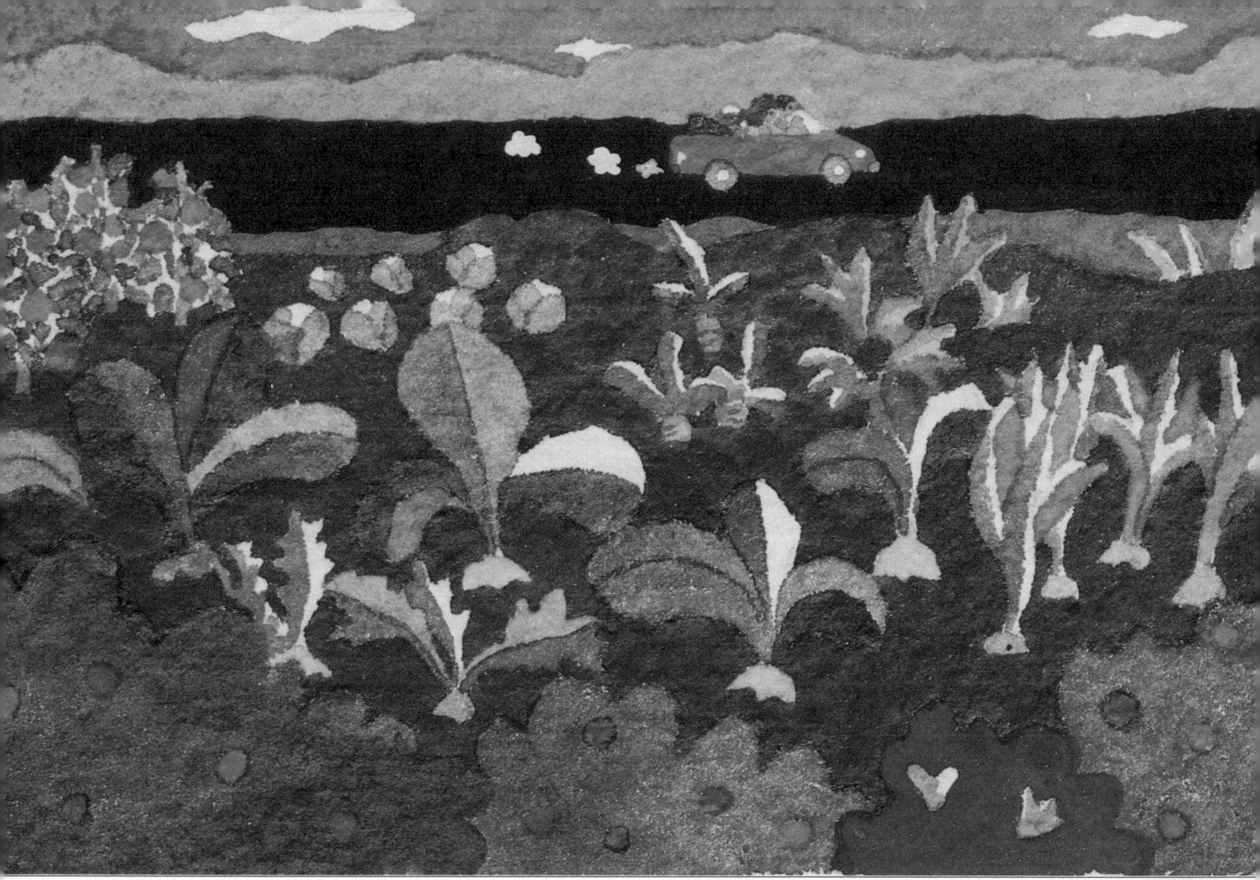

We go by a garden.

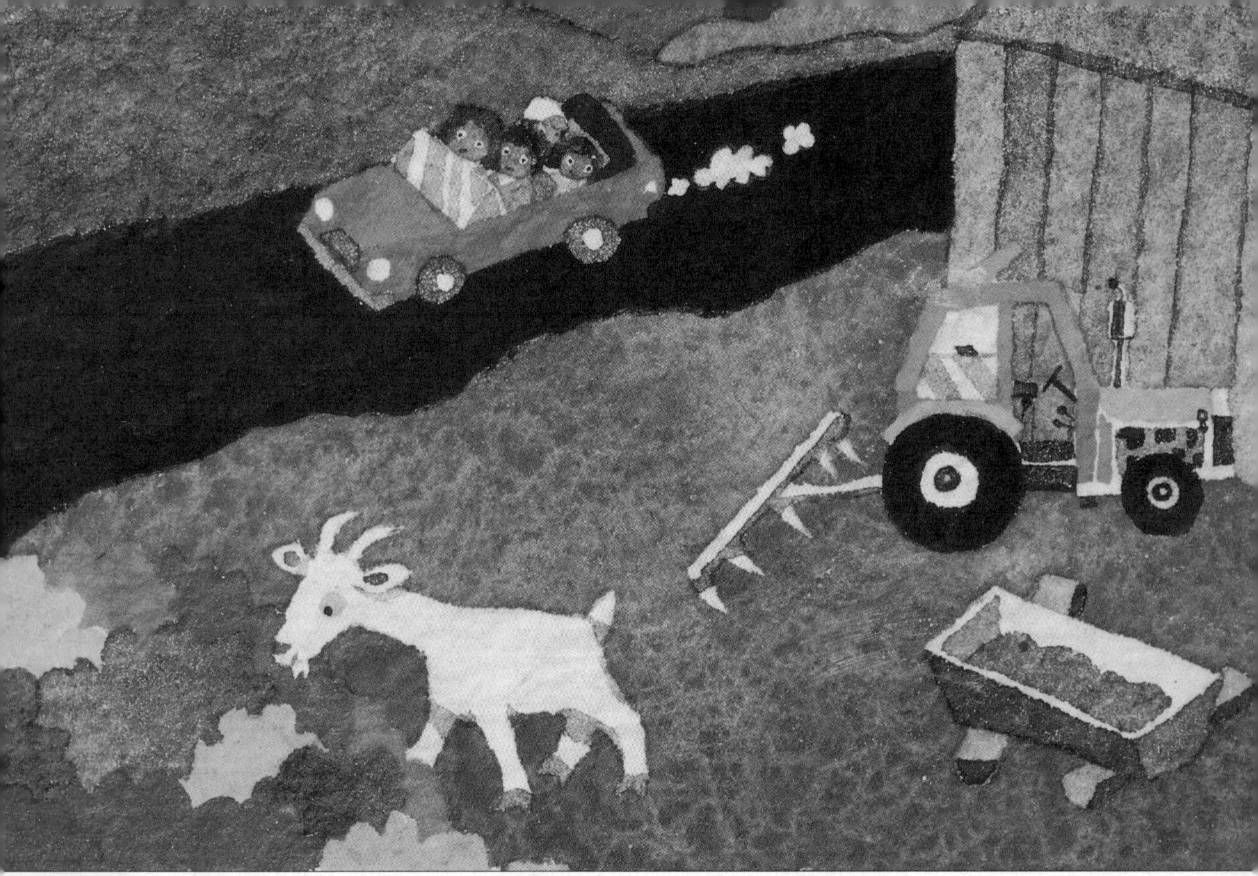

We go by a goat.

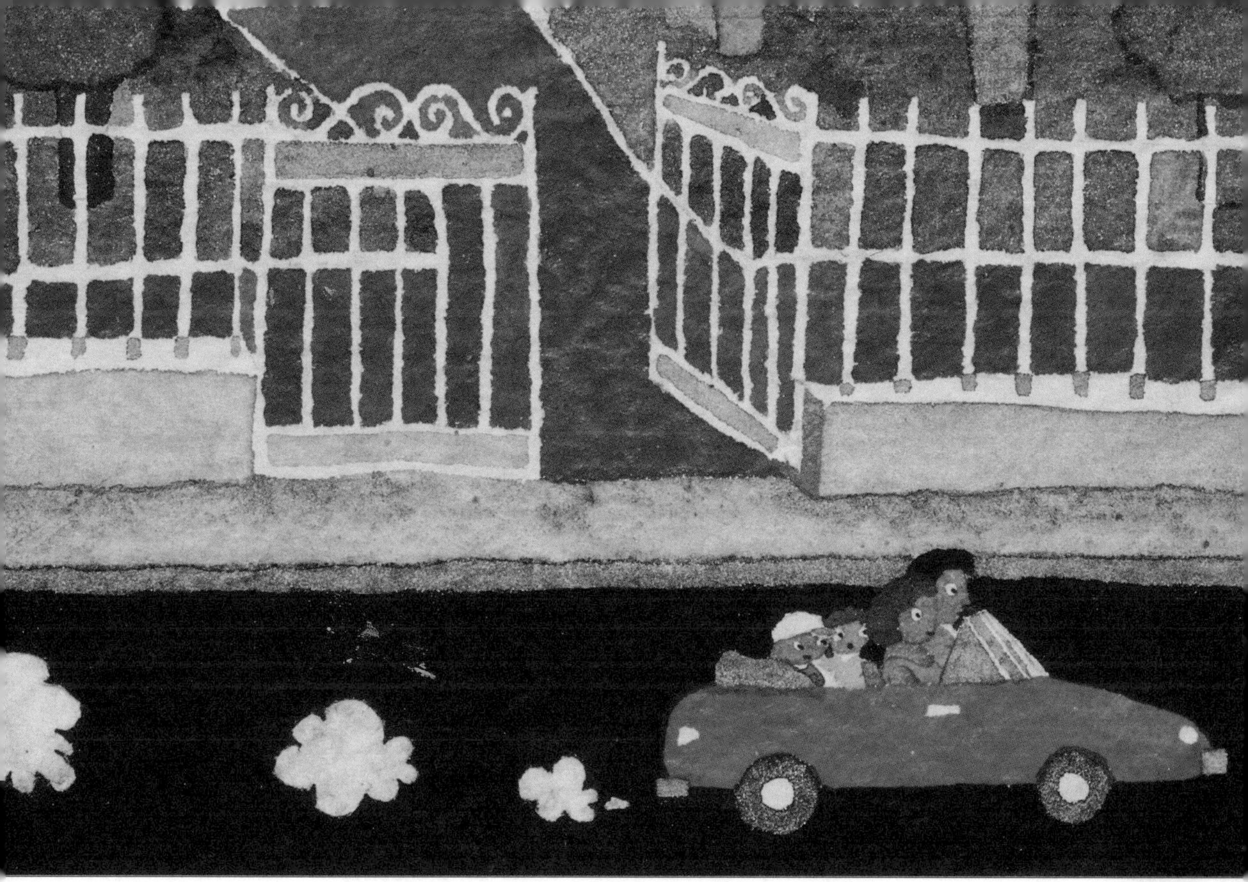

We go by a gate.

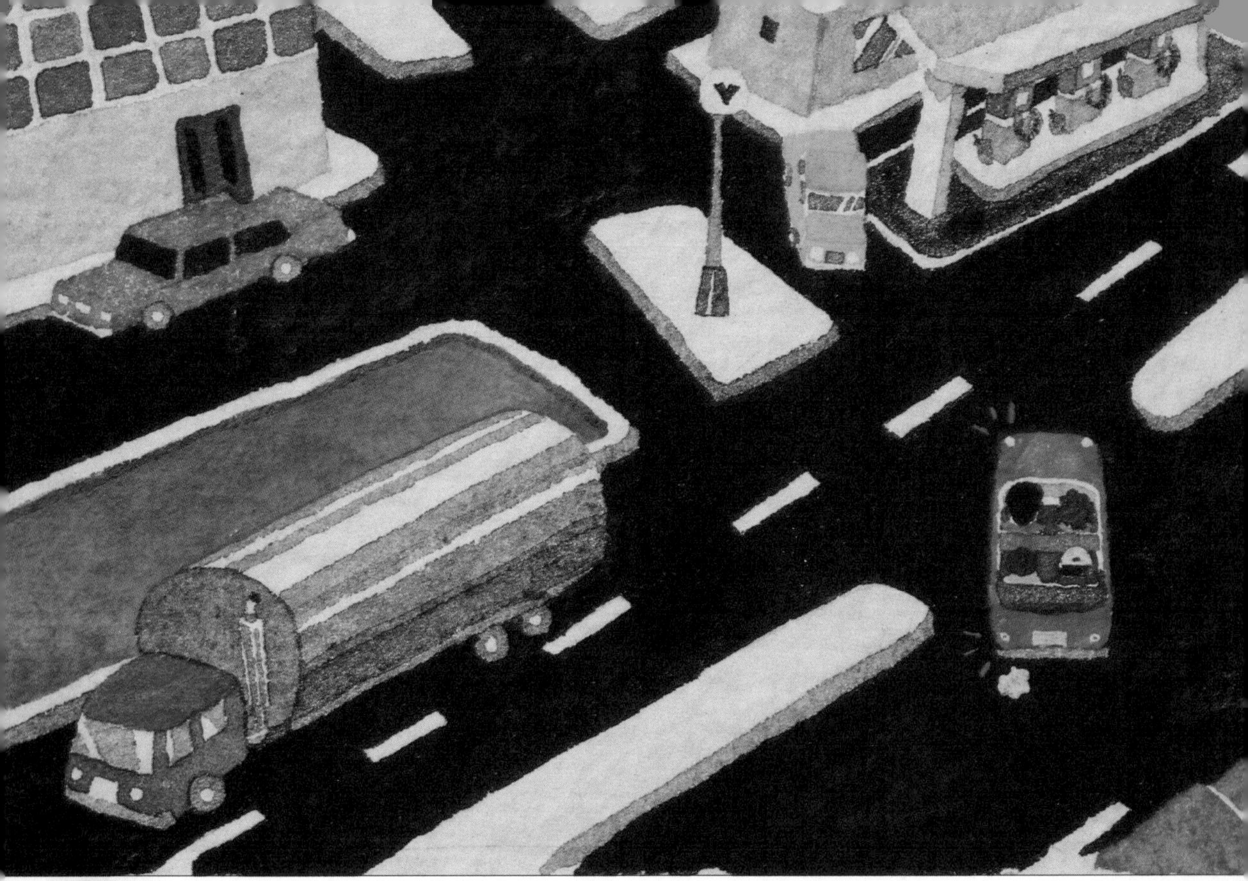

We go slowly.

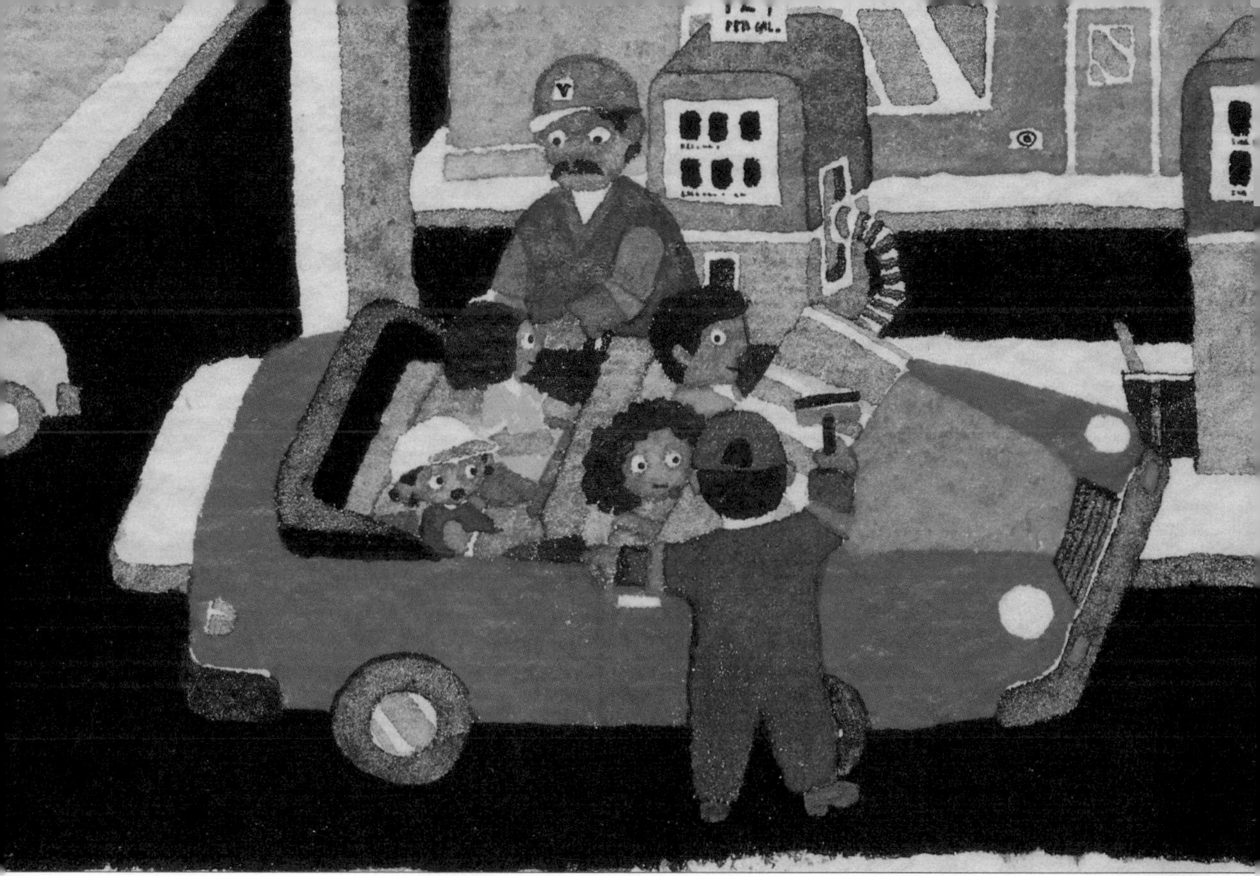

We get gas.

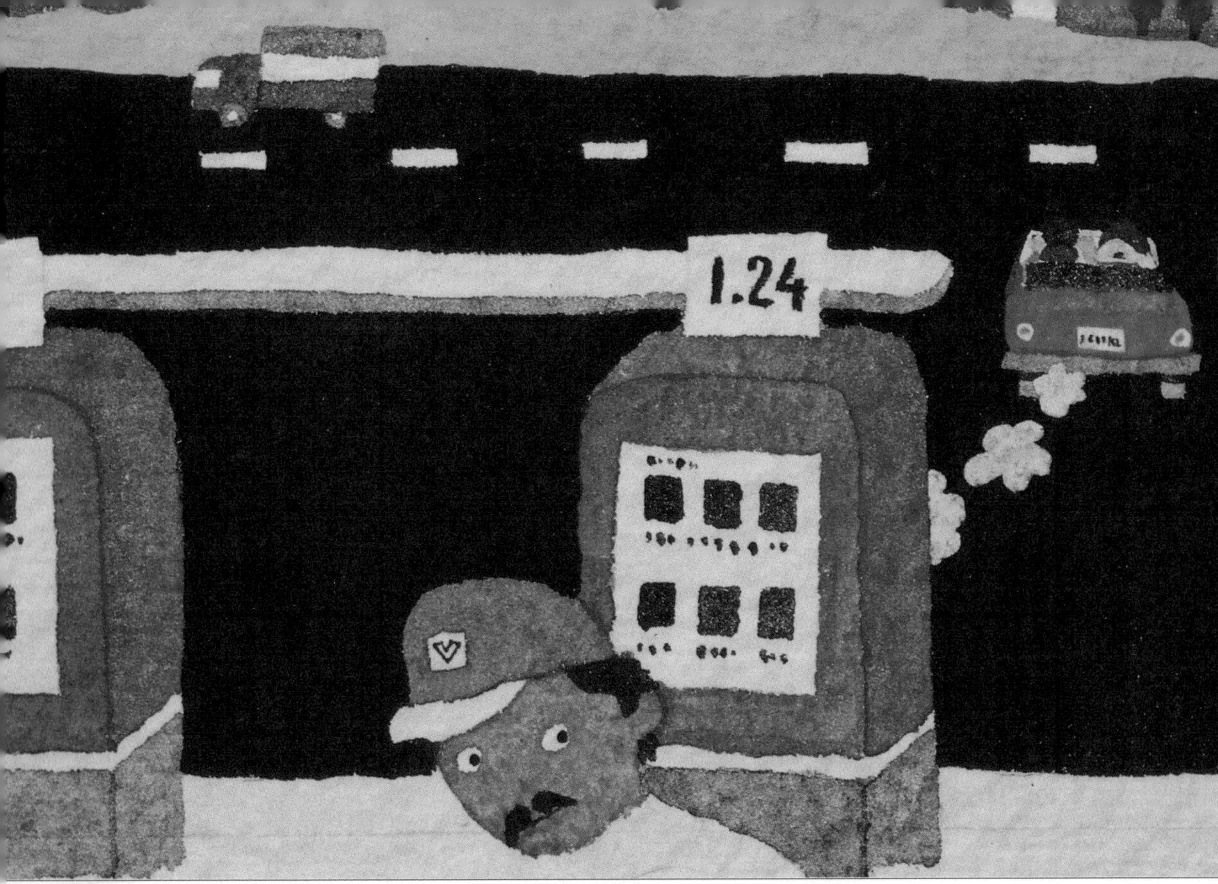

Let's go!